Fairy Mom and Me

Also by Sophie Kinsella

Finding Audrey

THE SHOPAHOLIC SERIES

Shopaholic to the Stars
Confessions of a Shopaholic
Shopaholic Takes Manhattan
Shopaholic Ties the Knot
Shopaholic & Sister
Shopaholic & Baby
Mini Shopaholic

OTHER NOVELS

My Not So Perfect Life
I've Got Your Number
Can You Keep a Secret?
The Undomestic Goddess
Remember Me?
Twenties Girl
Wedding Night

SOPHIE KINSELLA

Fairy Mom
and Me

illustrated by
Marta Kissi

Delacorte
Press

Text copyright © 2018 by Sophie Kinsella
Jacket art and interior illustrations copyright © 2018 by Marta Kissi

All rights reserved. Published in the United States by Delacorte Press, an imprint of Random House Children's Books, a division of Penguin Random House LLC, New York.

Delacorte Press is a registered trademark and the colophon is a trademark of Penguin Random House LLC.

Visit us on the Web! rhcbooks.com

Educators and librarians, for a variety of teaching tools,
visit us at RHTeachersLibrarians.com

Library of Congress Cataloging-in-Publication Data is available upon request.
ISBN 978-1-5247-6989-5 (trade)
ISBN 978-1-5247-7065-5 (lib. bdg.)
ISBN 978-1-5247-6990-1 (ebook)

The text of this book is set in 14-point Horley Old Style.

Printed in the United States of America
10 9 8 7 6 5 4 3 2 1
First Edition

Random House Children's Books
supports the First Amendment and celebrates the right to read.

For Rex and Sissy

Contents

Meet My Fairy Mom and Me   1

Fairy Spell #1: FIXERIDOO!   11

Fairy Spell #2: CUPCAKERIDOO!   43

Fairy Spell #3: BETTERIDOO!   79

Fairy Spell #4: REWINDERIDOO!   109

Family Activity Guide   141

Meet My Fairy Mom
and Me

Hi there. My name is Ella Brook, and I live in a town called Cherrywood. I have blue eyes and dark brown hair. My best friends at school are Tom and Lenka. My worst enemy is Zoe. She lives next door and she's my Not-Best Friend. She looks mean even when she smiles. You'll meet them all later.

And this is my mom. She looks normal, like any other mom . . . but she's not.

Because she can turn into a fairy.

All she has to do is shut her eyes tight, say "Marshmallow," . . . and POOF! She's Fairy Mom.

I love it when she's a fairy, because her wings shimmer like hundreds of rainbows. She wears a silver crown that shines like starlight. She can fly in the air and turn invisible and do all other kinds of real magic.

Plus, she just bought a new wand that is really cool. It's called the Computawand V5. It has magic powers and a computer screen *and* an Extra-Fast Magic button.

Most fairies have Computawands nowadays. They have Fairy Apps and Fairy Mail and even Fairy Games. Mom sometimes lets me look at the apps and games if I've been good. (But she *always* turns off the magic function first.)

When Mom is not being a fairy, her Computawand just looks like a normal phone. Which is good, because it is a big secret that Mom is a fairy. No one must *ever* find out. I'm not allowed to tell anyone, not even my friends.

Most of the time, Mom is a boss in an office. She is very good at it. She's also very good at telling bedtime stories and singing songs in the car. She's the best mom in the world.

Ollie is my little brother. He's only one year old and he can't turn into a fairy. Everyone says he looks like me, but he doesn't, because he's a baby and I'm not. He can't even speak properly. His favorite word is "weezi-weezi-weezi."

And here's my dad. He can't turn into a fairy either and he can't do magic. He says he can park the car instead.

Mom knows I'd like to be a fairy. She says that all the girls in my family turn into fairies when they're grown up, so one day I will too. I will have sparkly wings and my own Computawand. I can't *wait*.

Aunty Jo and Granny look normal, just like Mom, but they can turn into fairies too. Aunty Jo has a Computawand V5 just like Mom's. She can work the computer screen very fast, and she knows every single spell code. Aunty Jo is very good at magic.

Granny won't get a Computawand because she doesn't like anything that goes *bleep*. She still has an old-fashioned fairy wand with a star on top. She says it's never let her down yet, and she won Best Spell at the Fairy Awards with it, three times in a row.

Aunty Jo won Best Spell last year too. In fact, Aunty Jo has won lots of fairy prizes.

Mom hasn't won any fairy prizes.

I'm not allowed to start magic lessons yet, but I'm trying to learn anyway. Every week, Mom has magic lessons from Fenella, her Fairy Teacher, who talks to her on Fairy Tube. I watch with her and try my hardest to remember all the spell codes.

Mom tries very hard too. I'm sure she'll get better one day, but for now she's not very good at magic. You'll find out what I mean soon.

Here are some of the magic spells we have had fun with so far—and some of the trouble they've gotten us into!

Fairy Spell #1

FIXERIDOO!

The Fixing Spell Mix-Up
and the Fairy Dust

It began Saturday morning. We were having breakfast and Ollie grabbed the milk jug.

"Careful, Ollie!" Mom said.

There is no point in saying "careful" to Ollie.

"Put it down!" I said. I tried to get the jug, but Ollie wouldn't give it to me.

13

"Give me the jug, darling," Mom said to Ollie. She tried to take it from him, but Ollie hugged it tighter, like a teddy bear. Mom pulled his hands off, Ollie grabbed it again . . . and suddenly the milk was all over the floor.

"Weezi-weezi-weezi!" Ollie said.

"He doesn't know what he's doing," Mom remarked.

I think he *did* know what he was doing.

The milk ran all over the floor, under the chairs and into the corners of the room.

"Never mind," my dad said. "I'll pop to the supermarket."

"That will take too long," Mom said. "We need more milk right now."

She stamped her feet three times, clapped her hands, wiggled her behind and said, "Marshmallow," . . . and POOF! She was a fairy.

Every time Mom turns into a fairy, I stare at her in amazement. When Mom is a fairy, she is sparkly all over. She has beautiful shimmery wings, and when they move, they send little breezes around. Even her smile is more sparkly.

Mom took her Computawand out of her bag. As soon as she touched it, it started to glow and grew into a wand.

"Are you sure about this?" my dad asked.

"Of course I'm sure!" Mom said. "You know I'm getting better at magic every day."

Dad muttered something, but we couldn't hear him.

"What?" Mom asked.

"Nothing," Dad said. "Go ahead."

Mom pressed a code on the screen—*bleep-bleep-bloop*—then waved it and said, "Milkeridoo!"

In an instant, there was a cow in our kitchen. A great big brown cow with a bell around its neck.

"Oops," Mom said. "I don't know how *that* happened."

"Do you know how to milk a cow?" Dad asked.

"No!" Mom said. "Of course I don't!"

"Moo!" the cow said.

It tried to walk around, but there wasn't room. So it flicked its tail and knocked all the apples out of the fruit bowl. Then it broke

three of Mom's favorite cups with the pink flowers.

"Stop that!" Mom shouted, and she

steered the cow away. Then the cow pooed on the floor.

"For heaven's sake," Dad said.

"I'm sorry," Mom said. "I'll try again."

She pressed a different code on her Computawand—*bleep-bleep-bleep-bloop*—and shouted, "Milkeridoo!" for the second time.

The ceiling started to rain on us. It was brown rain and it went everywhere, all over our hair and our breakfast. I licked the rain off my chin.

"It's chocolate milk!" I said. "It's raining chocolate milk! Yummy! Can we have this every day?"

"No, we can't," Mom said. She looked up, annoyed by the brown rain. "I didn't want chocolate milk. And I didn't want a cow. I just want a bottle of milk. Stoperidoo!"

The rain stopped. Then Mom pressed another code and shouted, "Awayeridoo!" and the cow disappeared too.

Dad sighed. He squeezed some chocolate milk out of his hair.

"There's too much magic in this house," he said.

"But it should have worked! I don't understand what's going wrong," Mom said. "This Computawand is brand-new. It has an Extra-Fast Magic button." She pressed the button on her Computawand, and it bleeped. "Should I try again?"

"No!" Dad shouted. "I mean . . . why not go to the supermarket? We need to buy some other food anyway."

"But the supermarket is very slow," Mom said. "And I'm very busy today. I've got lots to do."

"Great haste makes great waste," Dad said.

"What does that mean?" I asked.

"It means if you hurry too much, things will go wrong. *Especially* if you use magic."

Dad can't do magic or fly. He says if you want to fly, why not get on a plane, like normal people?

But Mom isn't normal people. She's Fairy Mom.

When we got to the supermarket, I saw Tom and Lenka.

"Hey, Lenka!" I called. "Hi, Tom!"

Tom was pushing the shopping cart to the register for his mom. Tom is always doing kind things like that.

There was a lady doing face painting, and Lenka was having hers done like a butterfly, with silver glitter.

"Can I have my face painted like Lenka?" I asked. But Mom shook her head.

"Sorry, Ella, no time. Come on!"

We ran up the cereal aisle and Mom grabbed boxes of cereal. We were going so fast that Ollie laughed and waved his hands, as if he were on a baby theme-park ride.

In the fruit section they were giving out free samples. But Mom said, "Sorry, Ella, no time. Come on!"

We rushed around with our cart like runners in a race. Ollie sat in the front and Mom sang, *"Ollie in the cart! Ollie in the cart!"*

But when we reached the register, Mom stopped singing. She looked annoyed. There were *so many people*. They were all standing in lines, with full, full carts. One man had a whole cart of flour!

Tom and his mom were leaving with their bags. Tom saw us and he called, "Good luck! We had to wait *forever*."

"Honestly!" Mom said. "Let's speed things along."

I wasn't sure that was a good idea. "Don't you remember what Dad said?" I asked. "'Great haste makes great waste.'"

"Well, I have a lot to do today," Mom said. "We need to hurry up. . . ."

We went behind a rack of baked beans where no one else was. Very quietly, Mom stamped her feet three times, clapped her hands, wiggled her behind and said, "Marshmallow," . . . and POOF! She was a fairy.

Quickly she pressed a code on her Computawand—*bleep-bleep-bloop*—then pointed it at herself and said, "Invisidoo!" Then no one could see her except me. I can always see Mom when she's invisible because one day I will be a fairy too.

Mom pressed another code on her Computawand screen—*bleep-bleep-bloop*—and pointed it at the lady at the checkout. "Speederidoo!" she shouted.

At once, the lady started throwing things quickly into the shopping cart. "There!" Mom said. "That's a lot better."

A pineapple landed in the cart—thud! A bag of potato chips landed—crinkle! A chicken landed—crash!

After a minute, Mom said, "Let's speed things up even more."

"Isn't this fast enough?" I asked.

"The faster, the better," Mom said.

She pointed her Computawand at all the ladies and men in the aisles and pressed the Extra-Fast Magic button. "Speederi-deederi-doo!" she shouted.

All the ladies and men started throwing things into their carts. They went faster and faster and faster.

"Mom," I said, "I think this is *too* fast."

Eggs flew through the air and landed—*smish-smash!* Bottles of soda crashed down and exploded—*fizz-whizz!* A chocolate mousse fell on the floor—*split-splat-splot!*

Food was flying *everywhere.* The old man in front of me got a block of stinky cheese on his head. One lady got broccoli stuck in her ears. Ollie was covered in baked beans, and he laughed and laughed. A tub of ice cream landed—*splat!*—and someone's dog ran in super-fast and started licking it off the floor until a worker chased it out.

Then the lady at the register started throwing the bags of flour into the cart. *Boom! Boom! Boom!* They all burst open. Everything was covered in a big white powdery cloud. Everyone looked like snowmen.

I wanted to laugh, but I was worried. All the people were running around and screaming. Mom looked worried too.

"What do you think, Ella?" she asked. "What should I do?"

"Use the Fixeridoo spell," I said.

I had learned about the Fixeridoo spell from watching Mom's magic lessons with Fenella on Fairy Tube. The Fixeridoo spell is the spell you use when things have gone really, really wrong. But it's so powerful that the Fairy Rule Book says you can only use it once a week.

"Do you remember it?" I asked Mom.

"Of course I do!" Mom said. She pressed a code on her Computawand—*bleep-bleep-bloop*—and waved it.

"Fixeridoo!" she shouted. But nothing happened. "Fixeridoo!" Mom shouted again. "FIX-ERIDOO!"

Food was still flying around in the air. A muffin hit me on the head. "Ow!" I shouted.

34

"Ella, I can't fix it." Mom looked really alarmed now. "Help!"

"The Fixeridoo spell is easy-peasy!" I said.

I wondered if Mom was using the right magic spell code. She finds it hard to remember them all. She says her head is too full of other things she can't forget, like how to raise a family and hold down a job.

"What numbers are you pressing on the Computawand?" I called.

"Four-five-nine," Mom said. She looked flustered. "Isn't that right?"

"No, that's wrong! It's four-*nine*-nine!" I called. "Press four-nine-nine!"

"Oh!" Mom cried. "Now I remember." She pressed the code—*bleep-bleep-bloop*—and said, "Fixeridoo! Please? *Please?*"

This time it worked. Everyone slowed back down to normal speed. The gooey eggs flew through the air, back into their shells. The chocolate syrup slurped back into its container. The baked beans marched back into their cans, one by one.

"Well done, Mom," I said. "You did it!"

"No, Ella," Mom said. "*You* did it. You're going to be a fantastic fairy when you grow up."

And she looked so proud I felt a little glow of happiness.

The people weren't fixed yet. Some were

shouting and some were crying. One lady was lying on the floor, yelling, "Help! Help! The eggs are alive!"

"Time for some Fairy Dust," Mom said.

Mom keeps her Fairy Dust in her purse in a secret pocket. She took out a handful and sprinkled it, all silvery-shiny, over everyone.

Fairy Dust is very clever. It makes you forget all the magic you've seen. For ten seconds, all the people in the supermarket were very still. They had sort of gone to sleep. Then . . .

"Go!" Mom said, and they all woke up.

The supermarket was calm again. Everyone was smiling. And our shopping cart was at the front of the line.

Mom quickly stepped behind the magazine stand. I knew she was going to become visible again.

"Where's your mom?" the lady at the register asked. "You're not alone, are you, little girl?"

"Oh," I said. "Of course not. My mom is . . . um . . . well . . . she's . . ."

"Here!" said Mom, appearing beside me. She wasn't a fairy anymore. Her shimmery wings had gone. She was just Mom, and she winked at me. "Oh no, what *is* Ollie doing?"

Ollie had his thumb in his nose. He pulled out a baked bean and smiled and said, "Weezi-weezi-weezi!" And then he ate it.

* * *

On the way out, we passed a cafe. The sign said SPECIAL: BLUEBERRY MUFFINS—TODAY ONLY.

I love blueberry muffins. "Mom, can we stop and have a blueberry muffin?" I asked.

Mom opened her mouth, and I knew she was going to say "Sorry, Ella, no time. Come on!"

But she closed her mouth. She thought for a moment. And then she said, "Let's sit down and have a blueberry muffin. You deserve a reward for helping me out."

After we got our muffins, we sat at a table. That was when I saw my best friend Lenka and her mom walk in. Lenka said, "Look, Ella! I'm a butterfly!"

"Oh . . . really?" I hesitated. "Did you see anything *else* in the supermarket? Anything strange?"

"Strange?" Lenka asked. "No, there was nothing strange." And she went to sit with her mom with a confused look on her face.

I wanted to tell Lenka about how I had remembered the code and saved the day. But I couldn't tell her even if she promised she could keep a secret. Waiting to be a fairy is hard sometimes.

Mom squeezed my hand and I knew she understood.

"Well done, Ella," she said, and gave me a little secret smile.

Mom had a cup of coffee and I had hot

chocolate and Ollie had apple juice. I could see some silvery Fairy Dust in his hair. Mom gave me my drawing book and pens and I started drawing a picture of all the flying food.

As I drew, I was thinking about being a fairy. "Mom, do I *have* to be a fairy when I grow up?" I asked.

Mom looked surprised. "No, Ella, of course you don't *have* to. But would you *like* to?"

I thought about the cow pooing in the kitchen. I thought about the chocolate rain, and the woman with broccoli in her ears, and all the people screaming. I didn't want to make pooing cows and flying broccoli.

But then I thought about remembering

the right magic code. And it made me feel really pleased with myself.

"Yes," I said. "I do want to be a fairy. I will be the most awesome, super-cool fairy in the world." And I smiled at Mom and ate my blueberry muffin.

Fairy Spell #2

CUPCAKERIDOO!

Super-Speedy Magic for Tea

It was a Saturday, and we had invited my best friends, Tom and Lenka, for dinner. I've known Tom since I was a baby—we were even born in the same hospital to-gether. But Lenka and I only became friends after her family moved here last year and she started going to school with me. Her mom is very pretty and can make special Polish pancakes, which are yummy. Tom and Lenka are both my best friends because they like playing hide-and-seek and telling jokes.

My Not-Best Friend, Zoe, was coming over too, with her mom. My mom and Zoe's mom think Zoe and I should be best friends because we live next door to each other, but Zoe is my Not-Best Friend because she does mean things to me. At school this week, she "accidentally" spilled her water all over my lunch. I wasn't looking forward to seeing her.

But I *was* looking forward to dessert. Mom was having a Fairy Tube lesson with

her Fairy Teacher, Fenella. She was learning the cupcake spell.

"It's very simple," Fenella said on the Fairy Computer screen. Fenella has long, straight hair and rectangle glasses, and she *always* says everything is very simple. As she began to show my mom the spell, she waved her wand and said, "Cupcakeridoo!" Ten chocolate cupcakes instantly appeared on the screen.

"Cupcakeridoo!" Mom said, copying what Fenella did, but instead of cupcakes, ten *cups* appeared.

"Oh no," Mom said. "I don't know what to do!"

Luckily, I didn't want Mom to make the cupcakes by magic.

"Mom," I said, "I know magic is quick. But if you use magic, I won't be able to lick the spoon."

Mom looked at her Computawand, then back at me. "Good point, Ella," she said. "Let's do it ourselves."

We mixed flour, eggs, sugar, butter and cocoa powder. When I helped stir, I dipped my finger in the bowl for a quick taste. It was *so* yummy.

"Can I eat the whole bowl of cake mix?" I asked. "Please, please? Just this once, as a special treat?"

"No!" Mom said. "You can lick the spoon later."

She got out the icing and sprinkles. Then we heard a sound outside. It was people clapping.

"Let's go see what's happening," Mom

said. She picked up Ollie and we went outside.

Zoe and her mom were standing in their front yard. A lady in a pink jacket was giving Zoe's mom a big silver cup, and a man was taking a photo of them. Lots of people were watching.

"Well done!" the lady said to Zoe's mom. "You have won Perfect House of the Year. Your house is the tidiest house in the whole of Cherrywood! Now, everyone, come inside and see this lovely house!"

We followed the people into Zoe's house. Zoe's house is always tidy, but today it was *super tidy*. All the floors were shiny. All the windows were gleaming. There was no

mess anywhere. No toys, no books, no coats, *nothing*.

Our house doesn't look like that. Our house has lots of useful things, all just where you need them. Like Ollie's toys all over the floor and a pile of coats on the bench in the hall. There are books everywhere, because you never know when you might want a book. Or a newspaper. Or an old *Fairy Times* magazine.

"Goodness." Mom gulped, looking around the super-tidy house. "It's very neat. Maybe we should tidy up our house before the dinner party."

We went to congratulate Zoe's mom. She looked very pleased with her silver cup.

"We won the prize!" Zoe told us. "Our house came in first!"

"Congratulations," Mom said. "And we're looking forward to dinner later. We're making chocolate cupcakes for dessert."

"Delicious!" said Zoe's mom. "We love chocolate cupcakes, don't we, Zoe?"

"I bet they won't be any good," said Zoe. She said it very quietly, just to me, so our moms wouldn't hear. "I bet you don't even know how to make cupcakes."

I tried to walk away. Mom says that when people are mean you shouldn't listen.

But Zoe followed me. "I bet your mom will burn all the cupcakes," she said. "I bet you have to throw them in the trash."

I felt furious, but I didn't show it.

"We won't burn them," I said, and I walked very quickly back to Mom. "Let's go home and finish the cupcakes."

* * *

When we got back, we stopped in the hall. I looked at Mom, and Mom looked at me. Our hall wasn't as tidy as Zoe's. It wasn't gleaming or shiny or neat. But it was cozy.

"I *like* our house," I said.

"So do I," Mom said, and she laughed. Even so, I could tell she was worried. I didn't want Zoe to come and laugh at our messy house.

"Let's tidy it up a *bit*," I said.

Mom put Ollie down, and we tidied all the shoes away and we hung up Ollie's hat. On the floor, I found one apple core, one newspaper, one old paper bag and one gummy bear. We threw them all away. (I wanted to eat the gummy bear, but Mom wouldn't let me.)

"There!" Mom said. "Much better. Now let's finish the cupcakes."

But when we went into the kitchen, we both gasped.

"Oh no!" Mom said. "What's happened?"

Ollie had happened.

Ollie had gone into the kitchen. He had climbed up on a chair and pulled down the bowl of cake mix to play with. There was cake mix in his hair, on the floor, all over the cupboards and up his nose. He had pulled down the icing and the sprinkles. And he had jumbled up the newspapers on the table. The whole kitchen was a big fat mess.

"Ollie!" I shouted. "That was so naughty!"

"Weezi-weezi-weezi," Ollie said, and splatted some more cake mix on his head.

"Mom!" I cried. "What are we going to do? We'll never clean this up."

Mom smiled. "Of course we will!"

She stamped her feet three times, clapped her hands, wiggled her behind and said, "Marshmallow," . . . and POOF! She was a fairy.

"Which spell is best?" She
wrinkled her brow. "Let me think."

"Once, I was looking on the Spell App on
your Computawand," I told her, "and I saw
a spell called Cleaneridoo."

"Cleaneridoo!" Mom exclaimed. "Of course!
You are so clever, Ella."

I felt very
proud of myself
because I had
thought of the
right spell!

Mom pressed a code on her Computa-wand—*bleep-bleep-bloop*—and said, "Clean-eridoo!" She waved her Computawand. "Cleaneridoo!"

For a moment, nothing happened. Then, in the corner, the mop came alive. It whooshed over to Mom and stood waiting.

A moment later, the dustpan and brush came waddling over too. A bucket clanked along as well, and all the dishcloths jumped out of the sink and skipped over.

My mouth fell open.

"You've made the cleaning things *magic!*" I said.

"Yes." Mom looked pleased. "I've made them magic and super speedy. Now clean the floor," she told the mop. "Nice and quick. Off you go."

But the mop didn't move.

"No," it said in a moppy sort of voice. "I won't."

"*What?*" Mom stared at the mop. "*What* did you say?"

I gasped. "It talked!"

"Yes," Mom said. "And it wasn't supposed to. Mop, please stop talking and get to work."

"I won't," the mop said. "I want to play."

"Us too!" the cloths said in squeaky voices. "We don't want to clean. Cleaning is boring. Play! Play! Play!"

"You clean the kitchen right now!" Mom

said, raising her voice. When Mom goes to work, she is the boss of a big office, and she is used to people doing what she says.

"Won't!" the mop said, and it started dancing on the spot.

"I want to play too," said the dustpan in a kind of dusty voice. "Let's play hide-and-seek! One . . . two . . . three . . ."

All the cleaning things ran off and hid. The brush hid behind the bread bin. The mop hid behind Mom.

"Stop right now!" Mom said, but they didn't listen. So she turned to the table. "All right. Newspapers. *You* show the others how to behave. Tidy up! Tideridoo! Tidy up!"

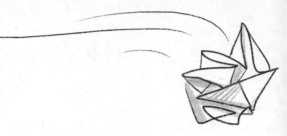

But the newspapers didn't tidy themselves. They crumpled themselves up and
started flying around like snowballs.

"Mom, the spell has gone wrong!" I cried.

"You've made everything *naughty*!"

Mom looked very red in the face. "Oh

no," she said. "I don't know how *that* happened. Let me try again." She pointed at the flour. "Flour! Tideridoo! Put yourself away in the cupboard."

The flour rose into the air and started flying slowly to the cupboard.

"There, you see?" Mom sighed with relief. "At least one thing is behaving nicely."

But then the flour tipped up and started pouring all over Mom, Ollie and me!

"No!" Mom shouted. "Bad flour!"

"Found you!" the dustpan said to the mop. "Now let's play Make a Mess!"

The brush started brushing all the food packages out of the cupboards. "No more cleaning for us! We love making a mess!"

"Bad brush!" Mom said.

"Play, play, play!" the cloths sang, dancing around. "Mess, mess, mess!"

"Stop it!" Mom cried.

"We love making a mess!" the cloths sang. "We love making a mess!"

I looked out the window and saw Zoe coming toward the house.

"Mom!" I shouted in a panic. "Zoe's coming! She'll see you! She'll see the mess! She'll see *everything*!"

I ran outside to stop Zoe from coming in. My heart was beating fast.

"Hello, Zoe," I said, and I stood right in her way.

"I've got a message for your mom," said

Zoe. "We can't come to dinner until a little later, because people are still taking photos of our house. We won Perfect House of the Year, you know."

"I *know*," I said.

"So where is your mom?" Zoe tried to walk forward, but I got in her way again.

"I don't know," I said. "Why don't you go home? Or . . . let's play in the back-yard."

"I need to give your mom the message," said Zoe.

She tried to walk past and I grabbed her arm.

"Let go!" shouted Zoe, and she ran past me into the house.

I ran after her and we both stopped dead in the kitchen.

Mom wasn't there. Neither was Ollie. All the magic had stopped. The flour had stopped tipping and the cleaning things had stopped dancing. The kitchen was quiet.

But it was very, very, *very* messy.

When Zoe saw the messy kitchen, her eyes got wide. She looked at the cake mix and the flour and the newspaper balls splattered everywhere. Then she looked at me and laughed her horrible laugh.

"This is the messiest house in the *world*," she said. "I'm going to tell my mom."

She ran away, back home. I felt hot and

prickly. We *don't* have the messiest house in the world. It was only a spell gone wrong.

A moment later, Mom came in. She wasn't a fairy anymore—she was just her normal mom-self, with cake mix smeared on her cheek and flour all over her hair. I wanted to laugh because she looked so funny. But I was a little worried too.

"Mom," I said with a wobbly voice, "did I choose the wrong spell?"

Mom gave me a big, tight hug. There was flour all over both of us, but I didn't care.

"You chose the perfect spell, Ella," she said. "I just need more practice. But for now, I'm going to give my wand a rest. Let's clean this mess up ourselves."

So we cleaned up. It was hard work, but we put on some music and chased each other around the kitchen with the brooms. Then we polished everything and pretended we were pirates cleaning our ship.

"Yo-ho-ho!" Mom said in a pirate voice. "Let's get this ship all shiny, sailor!"

"Aye-aye, Cap'n!" I called back.

Even Ollie rubbed the floor with a cloth.

At last the kitchen was clean, and it was nearly time for Zoe and her mom to come for dinner.

"You see?" Mom said. "We don't *always* need magic, do we? We can use our hands and brains too. That was fun, wasn't it?"

"Yes," I said, because it was. "But what about the cupcakes?"

"We don't need cupcakes. We've got lots of cookies." Mom opened a package and put a handful of oatmeal-raisin cookies on a plate. "Now go and brush your hair."

I brushed my hair and put on a sparkly fairy clip and imagined it was my fairy crown. I thought about being a fairy one day and all the spells I would do.

But I kept thinking about the cookies too. When I went into the kitchen, I knew I looked sad.

"Ella!" Mom said. "What's wrong?"

"We haven't got any cupcakes," I said.

"We don't need cupcakes to have dessert!"

"But Zoe said we would burn our cupcakes," I told Mom. "She said we'd have to throw them in the trash. And now she'll think it's true."

"She said that, did she?" said Mom, and she looked a little angry. But then she smiled. "All right, Ella, my darling. I promised you cupcakes, so we'll have cupcakes."

"But it's too late!" I said. Through the window I could see Zoe and her mom coming up the path.

Zoe was dragging her mom along. She was saying, "Just wait till you see their messy house. There's stuff all over the floor! *And* they haven't got any cupcakes!"

Very quickly, Mom stamped her feet three times, clapped her hands, wiggled her behind and said, "Marshmallow," . . . and POOF! She was a fairy.

Mom looked sternly at her Computawand. "No nonsense, now."

Suddenly the doorbell rang.

"Oh no, Mom!" I said. "They're here already!"

"Hold on!" she called. "Just coming!" Then she pressed a code on her wand—*bleep-bleep-bloop*—and said, "Cupcakeridoo!"

At once, the kitchen was full of cupcakes.

Hundreds of cupcakes. There were pink cupcakes and chocolate cupcakes and sparkly cupcakes, all on plates. There were even cupcakes that spelled out *Tom* and *Lenka* and *Zoe* and *Ella*. They were beautiful. And they smelled like the yummiest cupcakes in the world.

I was so amazed I couldn't speak.

"Toffee apple!" Mom said. This is what she says to stop being a fairy. Instantly her wings disappeared and she was back to normal again. She went to the front door and smiled at Zoe and her mom as she opened it.

"Come in!" she said. "Welcome to our dinner party."

When Zoe came into the kitchen and saw

all the cupcakes, her mouth dropped open.

"The house is looking beautiful!" Zoe's mom said. "So neat and tidy. And look at all these wonderful cupcakes! You could win the Perfect House of the Year Award!"

"I don't think our house is perfect," my mom said with a smile. "But we still love it. Don't we, Ella?"

Zoe looked at me with tiny angry eyes and gave me a push when she knew our moms weren't looking.

"I *know* the kitchen was messy," she said. "I *know* the cake mix was on the floor. How did you make all those cupcakes so quickly?"

But I didn't answer her. Instead, I thought about Mom and the talking mop.

I thought about the naughty flour and the dancing dishcloths and the newspapers flying like snowballs. I thought about polishing the kitchen and pretending to be a pirate. I thought about my best friends, Tom and Lenka, who would be arriving any minute. And I smiled my nicest smile.

"Here you are, Zoe," I said. "Have a cupcake."

Fairy Spell #3

BETTERIDOO!

How Not to Cure the Fairy Flu with a Bouncing Bed

One morning I went into Mom's bedroom and stopped in shock. She had red spots all over her face and was blowing her nose.

"Mom," I gasped. "I think you're sick!"

"I know," Mom said in a croaky voice. "I need some medicine."

Mom tried all the different medicines in

the cabinet, but nothing worked. Eventually, Dad had to call the doctor.

The doctor came and looked at Mom's spots. He took her temperature and looked in her ears.

"You have a very unusual kind of flu," he said. "You must rest and then you will get better."

"Rest?" said Mom.

"Yes," said the doctor. "Rest."

Mom doesn't like rest. She likes working hard and having fun and being busy. As soon as the doctor left, she got out of bed. She looked very wobbly, but she didn't want to show it. She stamped her feet three times, clapped her hands, wiggled her behind and said, "Marshmallow," . . . and POOF! She was Fairy Mom. But her wings were all dull and droopy, and her crown didn't shimmer.

"I am going to cure myself with magic," she told Dad and me.

"I think that's a bad idea," Dad said, looking alarmed. But Mom pointed the Computawand at herself and pressed a code—*bleep-bleep-bloop.* "Betteridoo!"

We all waited. But Mom's spots didn't go away and her nose was still runny. Her wings drooped even farther.

"Do you feel better?" Dad asked.

"No," Mom said. "I don't know what's wrong. I'm going to look at the Fairy Doctor App."

She started scrolling down her screen, searching for a spell. Just then, Granny came in.

"Of course, you have fairy flu," she said as soon as she saw Mom. "I'm afraid there is no spell for fairy flu. If you try to cure it with magic, you'll make it worse. You must drink hot lemon water. And you definitely must not try any more magic."

"You probably need a good rest too, like the doctor said," Dad said.

"I don't want a good rest," said Mom. "I want to get better." She looked very, very annoyed. "Toffee apple," she said, and went back to bed.

* * *

After lunch I went to see how Mom was feeling. She was sitting up in bed all alone in her nightgown, drinking hot lemon water and reading her Spell Book.

Mom hardly ever gets her Spell Book out. It's very old and the writing is very tiny and the pages are very thin. It was written hundreds of years ago by the Old, Old Fairies. Nowadays most fairies have Computawands to tell them their spells instead. And they use Spell Apps too sometimes. But even so, every fairy has a Spell Book. I can't wait until I'm old enough to have one.

"Why are you reading your Spell Book?" I asked. "Granny said you mustn't do any magic."

But Mom took no notice. "Here we are," she said. "I knew I'd find something! A spell to make you feel cooler. That's exactly what I need." She got out of bed, stamped her feet three times, clapped her hands, wiggled her behind and said, "Marshmallow," . . . and POOF! She was a fairy.

Then she pointed her Computawand at herself, pressed a code—*bleep-bleep-bloop*—and said, "Cooleridoo!"

At once, snow started falling on her head.

"Oops," Mom said. "I don't know how *that* happened. Stoperidoo!"

She pointed the Computawand at herself, but the snow didn't stop.

"Mom!" I said. "You'll freeze! And your head will turn into a snowball! Should I call Aunty Jo? Maybe she can help you."

"No!" Mom said, looking angry. "I don't need Aunty Jo. I can do this *myself.*"

Mom then continued flipping through the book. "Let me try something else," she said. "Here we are—a spell for strength. Strongeridoo!"

At once, Mom's arms changed. They got big and muscly, like a champion weight lifter's.

"Oops," Mom said. "I don't know how *that* happened. I wonder how strong I am."

She reached over and took hold of me with one hand, then lifted me up over her head.

"Help!" I cried.

"I'm really super strong," Mom said. "Isn't that cool?"

I felt very strange, balanced on Mom's hand, looking down at her head.

"Mom," I gasped. "I think you should stop doing magic."

"But I'm sure I can cure myself," Mom said, putting me down again. "I just need to find the right spell. Look, here's a cure for spots. Spotseridoo!" She pressed a code on her Computawand—*bleep-bleep-bloop*—and all her spots disappeared.

"There!" Mom said. "You see? It worked. I knew it would."

A moment later, the spots came back, but now they were bright green. They got bigger and bigger, until her whole face was green.

"Oh no," Mom said. "It didn't work after all."

Now Mom had muscly arms, a green face and snow falling on her head. I didn't think she looked at all better. I sat down on the bed and said, "Mom, why don't you just rest, like the doctor said?"

But Mom wasn't listening. "Here we are." She turned to another page in the Spell Book. "A spell for feeling bouncy. *That* will make me stop feeling ill." Mom pointed the Computawand at herself, pressed a code—*bleep-bleep-bloop*—and said, "Bounceridoo!"

Suddenly the bed gave a little bounce. I looked at Mom, and Mom looked at me. The bed bounced again.

"Oops," Mom said. "That's not what I meant by bouncy."

The bed gave a bigger bounce and I clung to Mom. Then it gave lots of bounces—*bouncy-bouncy-bouncy*. It was going higher and higher, up to the ceiling and down again. I felt as if we were on a trampoline.

"Mom!" I cried. "I think I'm going to fall off!"

"Hold on tight, Ella!" Mom said. "I'll try to stop it. Stoperidoo! Stop, you silly bed!"

But the bed was still bouncing. All of a sudden, it gave a huge bounce and flew toward the window. The window was getting bigger and bigger.

"What's happening?" I said.

"It must be part of the spell," Mom said. "Oh no. Hold on. . . ."

We sailed through
the window, then down
to the ground . . . and *bounce*.
We were outside, flying up into the
air. Then down again, and *bounce*.

The duvet was flapping.

I could feel wind in my hair. I shouted "Wheeee!" as we shot up again. Then I started laughing, because bouncing was *fun*.

"What are we going to do?" Mom said. "We can't just keep bouncing all day!"

The bed landed on someone's lawn, and then . . . *bounce*. Up we shot, into the air.

"Stoperidoo!" Mom shouted, but the bed didn't stop bouncing. We bounced ten more times. Then the bed seemed to get tired. It stretched and made a noise that sounded like a yawn. Then it landed on top of a house and stopped.

Mom and I looked at each other. We were stuck on the roof of a house. Neither of us had jackets, and Mom was even in her night-

gown. How were we going to get home?

"I'm really cold," Mom said. "I must get rid of this snow." She pointed the Computawand at herself and cried, "Heateridoo!"

But the snow didn't stop falling on her head. Nothing had happened.

"Oh no," Mom said. "I really wanted some heat."

Suddenly I heard a roar, and I screamed. A little red dragon was flying toward us. It had a pointed nose and sharp claws. It sat on Mom's shoulder and breathed out fire with a roary sound.

"Mom!" I said. "There's a dragon on your shoulder!"

"Not *that* kind of heat! Shoo!" she said to the dragon, but it wouldn't go.

"Can we keep him?" I begged. "Can we
call him Roary? I think Dad would love him.
You know I've always wanted a pet."

"Dad would not love him!" Mom said.

"We need to get rid of this dragon and get home!"

As I looked at the dragon, I spotted a man nearby. He was on the roof of the house next door, fixing the tiles.

"Look, Mom!" I said. "There's a man. He can help us."

"I'll talk to him," Mom said. "Excuse me!" she called, waving her arms. "Coo-eee!"

The man turned around. When he saw Mom, he nearly fell off the roof in shock.

"Help!" he shouted. "It's a monster! It's a monster with a green face and muscly arms and a dragon on its shoulder!"

"I'm not a monster!" Mom said, and the

dragon roared. The man looked even more scared.

"It can talk!" he said. "Help! Save me from the monster!"

"I'm not a monster!" Mom said. She looked a little upset.

"Please don't eat me," begged the man.

"I'm not going to eat you!" Mom said. "Why would I eat you?"

"Because you're a monster!" said the man.

The man looked so scared of Mom that I couldn't help giggling.

Just then I heard a voice behind me. "And *what* exactly are you doing?"

I turned around to find another fairy. It was Granny! *Fairy* Granny! She was flying

through the air with her shimmery wings
and gold crown with blue stones, frown-
ing. She sat down on the bed, fluttering her
wings.

"A giant butterfly!" said the man on the other roof. "Help! It's a giant man-eating butterfly!"

"Stilleridoo!" Granny said, and the man went very still and quiet.

Granny looked hard at Mom.

"Your husband called me and said that you and Ella were missing. He was very worried, and now I am too. What on earth are you doing out here? Why do you have a green face, muscly arms, snow falling on you and a dragon on your shoulder?"

Mom looked ashamed. "I thought I might find a magic cure for fairy flu," she said.

"There *isn't* a magic cure for fairy flu," Granny said. "I've already told you that. You just have to wait and be patient."

"I don't like waiting and being patient," Mom said.

"I know," Granny said. "Nobody does. But that's life. Now, I will clear up all your silly magic mistakes for you. And I will use Fairy Dust on all the people who saw your bouncing bed so they will think it was a dream. Including this poor man." She pointed to the man on the roof.

"Thank you," Mom said.

"And in return, you must promise me you will drink hot lemon water and *rest,*" Granny said. "Then you will get better."

"I promise," Mom said. "Thank you." Then she looked at her muscly weight-lifter arms. "Do you think I should keep these? They're so strong."

"No," Granny said. "You wouldn't fit into any of your clothes." She waved her wand and said, "Fixeridoo!"

A moment later, everything was right again. We were back in our house, on the bed. Mom just had ordinary red spots like before and normal arms and no snow falling on her. And she was asleep.

I looked all around, but Roary the dragon was gone too.

"Bye-bye, Roary," I said sadly. Then I put the Spell Book away and crept out of the room.

＊ ＊ ＊

A week later, Mom was better. Her spots were all gone. She got out of bed and had breakfast and put on her office suit to go to work.

When we went outside, Zoe's mom was in the garden. She was planting some bulbs.

"I am growing some daffodils," she told us. "They will be very pretty. But it will take a long time. We must be patient." Then she sighed. "I don't like being patient."

"Me neither," Mom said.

"Waiting is so boring," Zoe's mom said.

"Yes," Mom said. "It is. But sometimes waiting is better than rushing. Isn't it, Ella?"

I thought about Mom rushing to get better. I thought about her green spots, the snow and the bouncing bed and the man who thought she was a monster.

Then I smiled at her and I said, "Yes, Mom. Sometimes waiting is better than rushing."

Fairy Spell #4

REWINDERIDOO!

The Best Field Day Ever—
Again and Again . . .

One morning, Mom came to my room and gave me a pair of sneakers.

"What are those for?" I asked.

"For field day at school," she said. "You should practice your jumps before we go!"

I went out to the backyard and ran along the grass. I stepped, stepped, then jumped a couple times. But my shoelaces were too long, and during one of my tries I tripped over them and fell to the grass with a thud, bumping my nose. I'm not very good at sports, but Miss Allen says sports are supposed to be fun, so I knew I should try again.

But then my Not-Best Friend, Zoe, ran by in her new sneakers, pointing and laughing at me with her horrible laugh before running into her house.

I didn't say anything, because Mom says I should ignore people who don't have anything nice to say, but my face felt hot and I couldn't help but feel sad. I brushed the mud off my knees and tried to tie up my laces, but they got tangled in a knot. I hate shoelaces.

"Ready for field day?" I heard someone say. I looked up and saw Zoe's mom going into her house with some shopping bags. "Oh my, it looks like you're having some problems over there!"

As Zoe's mom went inside her house, my mom came out and saw me trying to tie my laces.

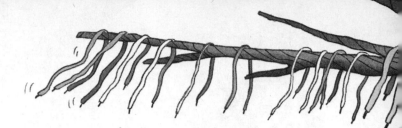

"Come on, Ella!" she said. "It's time to go. Let's fix you up."

She looked around to make sure no one could see. Then she stamped her feet three times, clapped her hands, wiggled her bottom and said, "Marshmallow," . . . and POOF! She was a fairy.

She pointed at my shoes with her Computawand. "Laceridoo!"

Suddenly my laces started moving on their own. But they didn't knot themselves neatly. They flew into the air and went to hang on the apple tree. Then all of my dad's shoelaces came flying out the window and

went to hang on the tree too.
They looked like spaghetti.
I started giggling.

"Oops," said Mom, and pressed her
Computawand. "I don't know how *that*
happened."

Then I spotted Aunty Jo walking up
the driveway. She was going to come and
watch me at my field day too. Aunty
Jo is very good
at magic. Her
house is full
of gold medals
from the Fairy

Awards. She saw the laces waving in the tree and shook her head.

"What a mess," she said. "Let me fix this for you." She stamped her feet three times, clapped her hands, wiggled her behind and said, "Strawberry shortcake," . . . and POOF! She was a fairy, just like Mom, with silver wings and a crown. Aunty Jo Fairy pointed her Computawand at the tree and said, "Fixeridoo!" At once my laces zoomed back into my shoes and tied a neat knot. All Dad's laces sailed back in through the window.

"Thank you, Aunty Jo Fairy," I said.

"Well done, Jo," said Mom, although she didn't look very pleased.

"My pleasure," said
Aunty Jo Fairy. "And
now, Ella, what about a little
Twinkletoes spell to make you
run nice and fast today?"

I liked the idea of
a Twinkletoes spell.

"Yes, please!"
I said.

But Mom stepped forward before Aunty Jo Fairy could point her wand. "No!" she said. "That's cheating! We do not cheat in this family. Do we, Ella?"

I knew Mom was right. Cheating was wrong. But I really, really wanted a Twinkle-toes spell to help me. Maybe then I could even win a race.

"It's just one tiny spell," Aunty Jo Fairy said to Mom. "Don't you want Ella to win all the races?"

"Not by cheating," Mom said firmly.

"Look!" I said. "Zoe's coming back. She'll see you!"

Mom and Aunty Jo Fairy stepped behind

a bush to hide. As Zoe reached our yard, she stopped. She squinted at the bush.

"What was that?" she said. "Is someone hiding?"

"No!" I said at once. "It's nothing. Maybe a squirrel."

"Oh." Zoe looked at the bush again, then

turned away. "Well, I'll see you at field day, Ella. Oh no, I *won't* see you. Because I'll be at the front of every race and you'll be at the back. You're going to lose every single one." She stuck out her tongue and ran off.

I was too upset to reply.

As Aunty Jo Fairy came out from behind the bush, she looked furious. "What a horrible girl!" she said. "Ella, if only I could give you the Twinkletoes spell. You would twinkle and whizz along like a rocket!"

"Mom, *please* can I twinkle and whizz?" I said. "Just in one race?"

"No," Mom said, looking sternly at Aunty Jo Fairy. "You must promise me you will not put any spells on Ella to help her win."

"All right," said Aunty Jo Fairy, crossing her arms.

"Not even a tiny one," said Mom.

"I promise!" said Aunty Jo Fairy. "Not even a tiny one."

But when Mom wasn't looking, Aunty Jo Fairy winked at me.

Field day was in the grassy area behind my school.

"Welcome to field day!" said Miss Allen. "Now, let's begin!"

All the parents were standing on the sidelines, watching the races. The first race was running, and my whole class was lined up. I reached down to touch my feet, but they didn't feel twinkly or whizzy—they just felt normal. Aunty Jo hadn't put a spell on me after all. She must have listened to Mom. I felt a bit disappointed.

"On your marks, get set . . . *go!*" shouted Miss Allen, and we all began to run. I was

running as fast as I could, and I looked around to see where the others were.

I couldn't believe my eyes. They were all running slowly. Really, really slowly. Even Zoe.

"Come on, Zoe!" her mom was shouting. "Faster!"

"I'm trying!" yelled Zoe. "My legs won't move!"

Zoe and all the other children in the race looked like slow-motion people on TV. They looked so silly that I started to laugh.

"Ella!" Aunty Jo shouted. "Run!"

I ran to the finish line with everyone else miles and miles behind me. I was the winner!

"Congrats, Ella!" Tom said once he made it past the finish line. He was panting and red in the face. "My legs felt so weird. I tried and tried, but I couldn't run fast."

"Great job!" said Aunty Jo, and gave me a huge hug. "You'll get a gold medal now!"

Zoe was furious. "How did *you* win?" she

hissed so nobody could hear but me. "It's not fair. *I'm* the best at running."

"You did wonderful, Ella!" said Mom, but she gave Aunty Jo a hard stare. "What happened to the others?"

"I have *no* idea," said Aunty Jo. "Now it's time for the long jump."

We all lined up in front of the long jump. It was a tray of sand, and the person who jumped the farthest would be the winner. When my gym class had practiced the day before, I fell so hard on my butt that everyone laughed. I hoped I wouldn't fall like that today.

My best friend Lenka was up first. Once she got ready, she ran to the sand tray, *step,*

step; then she jumped. But she jumped the *wrong way.* She jumped backward.

"Oh my!" said Miss Allen, looking surprised. "Lenka, you should have jumped forward, not backward. I'm afraid you don't get any score. Tom, it's your turn."

Tom ran toward the sand tray. *Step, step* . . . and then he jumped backward too!

Everyone started laughing.

"I don't understand!" Tom said. "I wanted to jump forward, but my legs just jumped backward!"

All the children kept jumping backward. All the teachers were calling, "This way! Jump *forward*!" Then it was my turn. I ran to the sand tray. *Step, step, jump!* I landed in the sand with a crash and Aunty Jo cheered.

"Very good!" said Miss Allen. "Since nobody else jumped the right way, you are the winner, Ella."

"Hooray!" yelled Aunty Jo, waving her arms. "Ella's the winner! Ella gets another gold medal!"

I didn't feel as happy as I had expected. I didn't feel like a *real* winner. I had only won because everyone else went backward.

"Wait!" Mom shouted. I was amazed, because Mom had become a fairy in front of everyone. She waved her Computawand and said, "Freezeridoo!"

Everyone except Mom and Aunty Jo and me went still. All the teachers and parents and children were like statues—and as I looked at them, I started to giggle. Tom was standing on one leg. Mr. Wilson, the principal, was scratching his head. Zoe had her finger up her nose.

No one could see or hear us.

Mom turned to Aunty Jo with an angry look on her face.

"What have you done?" she said. "You promised not to put a spell on Ella."

"I didn't put a spell on Ella," said Aunty Jo. "I put spells on all the *other* children. First a Slow-Down spell, then a Go-Backward spell. Aren't I clever?"

She winked at me, but I didn't know whether to smile back.

"No, you are *not* clever!" said Mom. "I told you not to use any spells. I never use magic at Ella's school."

"That's because—" Aunty Jo stopped.

"What?" Mom asked. "Because what?"

"Because you aren't very good at magic," Aunty Jo said.

Mom started breathing hard. I think she was trying not to get angry. But *I* felt angry.

"Mom *is* good at magic!" I said to Aunty Jo. "She can fly! And she can turn invisible! She's the best mom in the world!"

"Sorry." Aunty Jo bit her lip. "I didn't mean to say that."

"Maybe I am not as good at magic as you," Mom said to Aunty Jo. "Maybe I don't have any gold medals. But I try hard. And Ella tries hard at sports. And that is what field day is all about. Trying hard. Isn't it, Ella?"

I nodded, even though I still really wanted a gold medal.

Aunty Jo looked down at the grass. "I was wrong. I shouldn't have done any spells. And I shouldn't have been rude about your magic," she said to Mom. "I'm very sorry."

Then I had an idea. I remembered a spell I had seen on Mom's Spell App.

"Mom," I said, "can we start field day again? Can we use the Rewinderidoo spell?"

Mom's eyes sparkled at me. "That's a wonderful idea, Ella!" she said. "We'll go back to the beginning of the field day and start again *with no spells*. Okay?"

I nodded. "Okay."

"Okay," Aunty Jo said. "Good luck, Ella!"

Mom got out her Computawand and looked at it. Then she stopped.

"The Rewinderidoo spell is very tricky," she said. I could see she was nervous. "I've never done it before without help. I hope it goes right." Then she looked at Aunty Jo. "I wonder if . . ."

"Let's do it together," said Aunty Jo, and she winked at me. She stamped her feet three times, clapped her hands, wiggled her behind and said, "Strawberry shortcake," . . . and POOF! She was a fairy, with shimmering wings and a diamond crown and a shiny Computawand.

Together, Mom and Aunty Jo Fairy pressed the special code on their screens—*bleep-bleep-bloop.*

"Rewinderidoo!" they shouted together, and

everything started going backward. It was like when they do a rewind on TV. I could see Zoe running backward. I could see Lenka eating a cookie backward. Then I saw Tom blowing his nose backward. That made me laugh.

Suddenly the rewinding stopped. We were in the field, at the beginning of field day again. Mom and Aunty Jo were back to normal.

"Welcome to field day!" said Miss Allen. "Now, let's begin!"

This time, no one ran slowly or jumped backward. Zoe won three gold medals for running and I made myself clap hard when she went up to get them. Zoe is very good at running, even if she isn't a nice person.

Then it was the three-legged race. I was with Tom. Lenka was with Zoe. Our legs were tied together and we had to run in time with each other.

"Now, children, don't rush," said Miss Allen before the race started. "You have to work as a team."

When the race began, Tom and I started counting. "One-*two*. One-*two*." We weren't very fast, but we ran along in time with each other. I could hear Zoe yelling, "Hurry up, stupid!" to Lenka. The next minute, Zoe and Lenka had fallen over on the grass.

But Tom and I didn't look back. We didn't need to shout at each other, because we were friends and friends don't shout. We just kept on going "One-*two*, one-*two* . . ." until suddenly we had crossed the line. We had won the race!

Miss Allen gave Tom and me each a shiny gold medal. Aunty Jo and Mom waved their arms and cheered and hugged each other. And I felt really happy. I had won a race for *real* this time.

"Well done, Ella!" Tom said to me.

"Well done, Tom!" I said to Tom, and we both laughed.

"Let's go and get some ice cream as a treat!" said Mom. "Tom, you come too."

Then Zoe walked up to us. She looked at me with small, angry blue eyes and said, "How did *you* win a race, Ella? You're not good at sports."

I thought about Aunty Jo's magic spells. I thought about running faster than everyone

else, and jumping the right way when everyone else went backward. Then I thought
about winning the race with Tom, without
any magic at all. And I thought about Mom
and Aunty Jo doing the
Rewinderidoo spell
together.

"I won because
Tom and I are
friends and we worked
as a team," I said.
"That is the *best*
way to win." And
I put on my shiny
gold medal and
smiled.

Family Activity Guide

Reading a book together as a family creates a lasting bond and sparks good conversation between parents and their children. *Fairy Mom and Me* is funny and entertaining, and raises important lessons about patience and teamwork. The discussion questions below are intended to promote creative and critical thought, and should be used after the book has been read in its entirety.

DISCUSSION QUESTIONS

1. Ella's worst enemy is Zoe. Discuss what Zoe does to Ella that makes them enemies. Talk about ways to deal with kids like Zoe.

2. What is "cool" about Ella's mom? How is Ella a "cool" kid? What do you like best about their relationship? How do Ella and her mom reveal their true character at the end of the novel?

3. Explain why Ella's mother turns off the magic function on the games and apps when Ella is

playing with the Computawand V5. At what age do you think Ella should be allowed to use the magic functions?

4. The fact that Ella's mom is a fairy must be kept secret. What might happen if others find out the truth about her mom's magical abilities?

5. How does Ella's dad doubt his wife's ability to perform magic? Why does he think there is "too much magic" in the house? How might he react when Ella is old enough to become a fairy?

6. Which of the "spells gone wrong" is the funniest? How does Ella help her mom when the spells are out of control?

7. What is the purpose of Fairy Dust? Explain what might have happened in the grocery story had Ella's mom not used Fairy Dust.

8. Ella and her mom work together to clean the kitchen after Ollie makes a mess. Ella's mom says, "We don't *always* need magic, do we?" (p. 72). What is the magic in working together

to complete a task? How might this apply in your own family?

9. Ella's mother attempts to cure herself of the fairy flu. What goes wrong? Explain Granny's reaction.

10. Ella's mom is an impatient fairy. How is patience a part of life? Relate a time when impatience has made life complicated for you.

11. How is Aunty Jo better at magic than Ella's mom? Debate whether Ella's mom is jealous of Aunty Jo. What happens when Aunty Jo misuses magic?

12. Ella's mom tells Aunty Jo that using magic to help Ella win at field day is "cheating." Discuss whether the same argument could have been used with Ella's mom when she tried to use magic in the supermarket to speed up the checkout line.

13. Define friendship from Ella's point of view. Describe Ella and Tom's friendship. How does

their friendship promote teamwork? Discuss how teamwork helps them win the three-legged race at field day.

FAMILY ACTIVITIES

Choose the activities most suitable for your family.

1. Together, write a sentence that appropriately describes each chapter title.

2. Create a job description for a Fairy Teacher like Fenella. Are there special qualifications? (For example, "Must be proficient at working the Computawand V5.") Is there required attire? What are the working hours?

3. The Fairy Rule Book states that a fairy can only use the Fixeridoo spell once a week. Make an illustrated Fairy Rule Book for Ella's mother. Include at least ten rules and spells.

4. Think about what happens when Ella's mother tries to cure herself of the fairy flu. Make a short video about the flying bed story

as told by the man on the roof to be aired on the nightly news of a Cherrywood television station.

5. Think about how fairies move. How do they walk or run? Do they dip and sway? Are they graceful? How do they use their arms and hands? Then choreograph a Fairy Dance to appropriate music. Use scarves and other accessories around the house to make a Fairy Dance costume.

6. As a family, read aloud several fairy tales. Note the following elements of a typical fairy tale:

> Often begins with "Once upon a time"
> Happens in the past
> Has a problem to be solved
> Features both good and evil characters
> Things often happen in threes
> Features an element of magic
> Ends happily ever after

Then choose a favorite part of *Fairy Mom and Me* and tell it as a fairy tale. Embellish it to include the above elements.

7. Make a pair of fairy wings that Granny might give to Ella when she grows up and becomes a fairy.

8. Make a fairy necklace for Ella using beads, pipe cleaners, glitter, or other fun materials found around the house.

9. Bake cookies in the shape of a magic wand that Aunty Jo might bring to Ella's house to celebrate her medal at field day. Decorate the cookies with Fairy Dust made with colored sugar or sprinkles.

10. Create a Fairy Garden using items found around the house. There are numerous sites on the Internet that give step-by-step instructions. The following is especially helpful: youtube.com/watch?v=IZlyWoW7Rww.

FINDERIDOO!

Can you spot Fairy Mom's favorite things
in the word search?

(Answers on the next page)

C	O	M	P	U	T	A	W	A	N	D	C
M	S	L	L	E	P	S	Y	T	W	Z	U
I	A	B	K	G	T	G	R	U	W	V	P
A	G	R	H	G	R	M	I	B	D	U	C
I	V	R	S	A	Y	E	A	E	R	I	A
R	C	T	N	H	I	D	F	L	G	E	K
Y	S	N	C	J	M	C	D	A	N	A	E
T	Y	T	T	H	O	A	M	A	V	P	U
U	L	U	E	X	Z	Z	L	H	D	V	K
B	F	L	L	I	N	O	L	L	I	E	P
E	H	U	L	W	Z	Y	T	D	O	X	B
O	C	M	A	B	D	R	J	T	P	W	E

COMPUTAWAND   FAIRY TUBE

CUPCAKE   MAGIC

DADDY   MARSHMALLOW

ELLA   OLLIE

GRANNY   SPELLS

C	O	M	P	U	T	A	W	A	N	D	C
M	S	L	L	E	P	S	Y	T	W	Z	U
F	A	B	K	G	T	G	R	U	W	V	P
A	G	R	H	G	R	M	I	B	D	U	C
I	V	R	S	A	Y	E	A	E	R	I	A
R	C	T	N	H	I	D	F	L	G	E	K
Y	S	N	C	J	M	C	D	A	N	A	E
T	Y	T	T	H	O	A	M	A	V	P	U
U	L	U	E	X	Z	Z	L	H	D	V	K
B	F	L	L	I	N	O	L	L	I	E	P
E	H	U	L	W	Z	Y	T	D	O	X	B
O	C	M	A	B	D	R	J	T	P	W	E

For a little more magic, read

Fairy Mom and Me #2
Fairy-in-Waiting

About the Author

SOPHIE KINSELLA is a bestselling author. The adventures of Ella and Fairy Mom are her first stories for children. Her books for grown-ups have sold over thirty-eight million copies worldwide and have been translated into more than forty languages. They include the Shopaholic series and other titles, such as *Can You Keep a Secret?* and *The Undomestic Goddess,* and *Finding Audrey* for young adults.

Adults (including Fairy Moms everywhere) can follow her on social media:

🐦 @KinsellaSophie

📘 SophieKinsellaOfficial

📷 sophiekinsellawriter

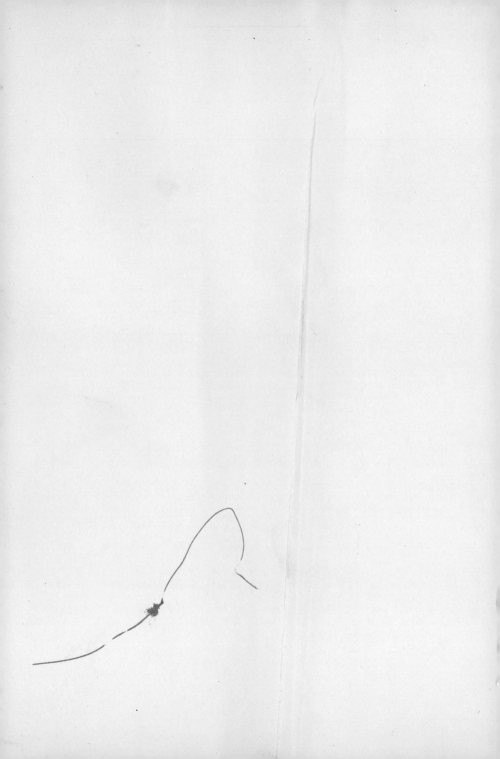